*Samuel French Acting Edition*

I0591774

# Girlfriend

*Book by*
Todd Almond

*Music & Lyrics by*
Matthew Sweet

# ∥SAMUEL FRENCH∥

**SAMUELFRENCH.COM**     **SAMUELFRENCH.CO.UK**

Book Copyright © 2016, 2017 by Todd Almond
Music & Lyrics Copyright© 2016, 2017 by Matthew Sweet
Music published by EMI Blackwood Music Inc.
Courtesy of Sony/ATV Music Publishing
All Rights Reserved

*GIRLFRIEND* is fully protected under the copyright laws of the United States of America, the British Commonwealth, including Canada, and all other countries of the Copyright Union. All rights, including professional and amateur stage productions, recitation, lecturing, public reading, motion picture, radio broadcasting, television and the rights of translation into foreign languages are strictly reserved.

ISBN 978-0-573-70575-5

www.SamuelFrench.com
www.SamuelFrench.co.uk

---

## FOR PRODUCTION ENQUIRIES

### UNITED STATES AND CANADA
Info@SamuelFrench.com
1-866-598-8449

### UNITED KINGDOM AND EUROPE
Plays@SamuelFrench.co.uk
020-7255-4302

Each title is subject to availability from Samuel French, depending upon country of performance. Please be aware that *GIRLFRIEND* may not be licensed by Samuel French in your territory. Professional and amateur producers should contact the nearest Samuel French office or licensing partner to verify availability.

---

CAUTION: Professional and amateur producers are hereby warned that *GIRLFRIEND* is subject to a licensing fee. Publication of this play(s) does not imply availability for performance. Both amateurs and professionals considering a production are strongly advised to apply to Samuel French before starting rehearsals, advertising, or booking a theatre. A licensing fee must be paid whether the title(s) is presented for charity or gain and whether or not admission is charged. Professional/Stock licensing fees are quoted upon application to Samuel French.

No one shall make any changes in this title(s) for the purpose of production. No part of this book may be reproduced, stored in a retrieval system, or transmitted in any form, by any means, now known or yet to be invented, including mechanical, electronic, photocopying, recording, videotaping, or otherwise, without the prior written permission of the publisher. No one shall upload this title(s), or part of this title(s), to any social media websites.

For all enquiries regarding motion picture, television, and other media rights, please contact Samuel French.

## MUSIC USE NOTE

Licensees are solely responsible for obtaining formal written permission from copyright owners to use copyrighted music in the performance of this play and are strongly cautioned to do so. If no such permission is obtained by the licensee, then the licensee must use only original music that the licensee owns and controls. Licensees are solely responsible and liable for all music clearances and shall indemnify the copyright owners of the play(s) and their licensing agent, Samuel French, against any costs, expenses, losses and liabilities arising from the use of music by licensees. Please contact the appropriate music licensing authority in your territory for the rights to any incidental music.

## IMPORTANT BILLING AND CREDIT REQUIREMENTS

If you have obtained performance rights to this title, please refer to your licensing agreement for important billing and credit requirements.

*Girlfriend* was originally produced by
Berkeley Repertory Theatre, Berkeley, CA
Tony Taccone, Artistic Director / Susan Medak, Managing Director
Developed with the assistance of Director Patrick Trettenero

**GIRLFRIEND** received its world premiere at the Berkeley Reparatory Theatre (Tony Taccone, Artistic Director; Susan Medak, Managing Director) in Berkeley, California on April 9, 2010. The director was Les Waters, with choreography by Joe Goode, and musical direction by Julie Wolf. The scenic and costume designer was David Zinn, the lighting designer was Japhy Weideman, and the sound designer was Jake Rodriguez. The production stage manager was Michael Suenkel. The cast was as follows:

| | |
|---|---|
| **WILL**............................................................... | Ryder Bach |
| **MIKE** ............................................................... | Jason Hite |

**GIRLFRIEND** was presented at the Actors Theatre of Louisville (Les Waters, Artistic Director; Kevin E. Moore, Managing Director) in Louisville, Kentucky on January 29, 2013. It was directed by Les Waters, with choreography by Joe Goode, and musical direction by Julie Wolf. The scenic and costume designer was David Zinn, the lighting designer was Mark Barton, and the sound designer was Jake Rodriguez. The production stage manager was Paul Mill Holmes. The cast was as follows:

| | |
|---|---|
| **WILL**............................................................... | Ryder Bach |
| **MIKE** ............................................................... | Curt Hansen |

**GIRLFRIEND** was presented at the Kirk Douglas Theatre by Center Theatre Group (Michael Ritchie, Artistic Director; Stephen D. Rountree, Managing Director) in Los Angeles, California on July 12, 2015. It was directed by Les Waters, with choreography by Joe Goode, and musical direction by Julie Wolf. The scenic and costume designer was David Zinn, the lighting designer was Ben Stanton, and the sound designer was Jake Rodriguez. The production stage manager was Paul Mill Holmes. The cast was as follows:

| | |
|---|---|
| **WILL**............................................................... | Ryder Bach |
| **MIKE** ............................................................... | Curt Hansen |

# CHARACTERS

**WILL** – any race, any ethnicity

**MIKE** – any race, any ethnicity

# AUTHOR'S NOTES

The plot of *Girlfriend* is a bit hidden in the script, but it's there. It's the long, slow, agonizing way these two boys inch toward each other. They're midwestern, so they always engage in polite conversation, but subtextually, they are in agony and searching for clues from each other. I've seen a couple of run-throughs in rehearsals where the actors let the inner turmoil drop and play the scenes as if these two boys just really like each other and are having a great time together, and it makes the piece, honestly, a bit insufferable. It takes away the plot and becomes a series of scenes with no tension. The boys are in agony, which we find amusing!

A couple of things to remember: This piece takes place before the internet and before there were any real gay characters on television. (Sandra Bernhard was just playing a lesbian on *Roseanne*, which was mind-blowing to me. So dangerous.) Will truly thinks he's the only gay person in Nebraska, maybe the world. And there was no gay-chic cachet at that time. Being gay was not cool – let's recall that Matthew Shepard was killed in 1998 in Laramie, Wyoming, which is very near Alliance, Nebraska. So Will and Mike have a lot to fear, and they must be very careful with what they reveal, even to each other. Even though it is clear to us, the audience, what is happening, these boys live in doubt and secrecy (is this all a set-up? Is he going to call me a faggot?), and so the bloom of their love is a s-l-o-w bloom – and because that very bloom is the plot, it should be calibrated carefully. Ultimately, these are just two young people falling in love for the first time; an experience not exclusive to gayness, but the added anxiety of gayness and all that it entails in 1990s small-town America is what makes *Girlfriend, Girlfriend.*

The dialogue has a lot of ellipses [...] – these are meant to indicate either a struggle finding the right words or a midwestern trailing-off. It's rarely if ever an interruption by the other character. Don't be afraid of awkward silences, pauses, lack of eye contact, or moments of uncertainty. Mike and Will are nervous and normal and they are reading the clues beneath the lines. They haven't developed their adult identities yet, and so sparkling conversation is not an option. They doubt themselves most of the time and slowly find confidence in each other.

A thought about the design: Wonderful Les Waters directed the original production with scenic and costume design by David Zinn. I loved the simplicity. Mike's couch was his car and his bed (a hilariously drawn-out moment of Mike pulling the hide-a-bed out for the "Your Sweet Voice" scene still makes me laugh), and a simple wall felt like a movie screen and an old building in downtown Alliance. These choices worked well, as it really made the world reduce to just these two boys and their simple lives. Another choice that I loved was the all-girl rock band in a shag-carpeted rock-band rehearsal space. It was genius – this kind of riot grrrl power, self-possessed and proud-to-be-queer energy supporting these boys in their struggle. I recommend this choice. Julie Wolf led the band, and they rocked.

What else? Let the piece take its time. It has two climaxes: The kiss at the end of Act One – Don't take an intermission! – and then the "break-up" at the end of Act Two. *Girlfriend* is as much about taking one's first steps into adulthood (in Mike's case, with a plan; and in Will's case, with no plan at all) as it is about that first love, that first kiss, and the music that got inside of you the deepest because your heart was so exposed.

I love Matthew Sweet's music, and these boys do too. It speaks for them in the way that music does when you are a teenager.

# ACT I

*(Alliance, Nebraska. The summer after high school graduation, 1993.)*

*(The set should be simple, invoking the wide-open plains of Nebraska.)*

## [MUSIC NO. 01 "OVERTURE"]

*(The **BAND** members enter and take their places. They check mics, tune, etc. They launch into the intro of the song. As it reaches its climax, the lights shift and...)*

### Scene One

*(…**WILL** enters. He has a backpack over his shoulder. He goes immediately to a large trash can, removes the lid, takes the backpack from his shoulder, unzips it, pulls from it a well-used textbook, and holds it tauntingly over the open bin. He looks at us.)*

**WILL.** Today is New Year's Day. I lied. It's June 18. But I'm calling it New Year's Day. High school – over!

*(He drops the book into the trash can.)*

Happy New Year!

*(He's genuinely tickled by this. He pulls another book from his backpack and holds it above the trash can.)*

This year, I resolve to drop my bad habit of learning things.

*(He drops the book into the trash can.)*

Yay!

*(He pulls out a fiv-subject notebook that's stuffed with papers. He holds it above the trash can.)*

Should Old Acquaintance Be Forgot?

*(He drops it in the trash can.)*

Yes!

*(He looks at the back pack and thinks, "What the hell," and he drops the entire bag in the trash can.)*

Yay!

*(He looks around, a big smile on his face.)*

Hello, Freedom. I was walking home from school for the last time, and I swear to God every lawn had just been cut. I thought, this is what the world will now smell

like. Every day... *(Suddenly, he remembers something.)*
Oh! Oh, oh, oh!

> *(He retrieves the backpack from the trash,
> frantically searches through it. Meanwhile,
> **MIKE**, also wearing a backpack, enters in a
> different space. He removes the books from
> his backpack and puts them neatly into a
> cardboard box. **WILL** finds what he's looking
> for, a homemade mix-tape, which he proudly
> shows us. He then puts it into the stereo. At
> the same time, **MIKE** puts a CD in his stereo.
> They both press play.)*

### [MUSIC NO. 02 "I'VE BEEN WAITING"]

> *(**MIKE** sings [he's singing along to the CD, but
> we hear only his voice and the **BAND**, live].
> **WILL** listens to the tape – it's the same song
> that **MIKE** is listening to.)*

**MIKE.**

WHEN YOU SAID TO ME, "YOU ARE NOT SO OLD."
DID I KNOW IT THEN, 'CAUSE I HAD JUST BEEN TOLD

I DIDN'T THINK I'D FIND YOU

| **MIKE.** | **BACKUPS.** |
|---|---|
| PERFECT IN SO MANY WAYS | |
| BUT I'VE BEEN WAITING | WAITING |
| AND I WANT TO HAVE YOU | HAVE YOU |
| I'VE BEEN WAITING | WAITING |

**MIKE.**

AND I WANT TO

> *(**WILL** laughs, like he's finally just understood
> a joke he was told. He looks at us.)*

**WILL.** Wow. This *is* good. Michael said I would like it.
*Michael.*
Michael is his name. He's... *(Sigh.)* ...And...doesn't it
smell like freshly-cut grass in here?!

> *(**WILL** dances around to the following verse.)*

**MIKE.**
> THE SECRET ON YOUR LIPS
> THAT NOBODY KNOWS
> GENTLE IN YOUR EYES
> YOU CAN WEAR MY CLOTHES YOU KNOW

| **MIKE & WILL.** | **BACKUPS.** |
|---|---|
| I DIDN'T THINK I'D FIND YOU | |
| PERFECT IN SO MANY WAYS | |
| AND I'VE BEEN WAITING | WAITING |
| AND I WANT TO HAVE YOU | HAVE YOU |
| I'VE BEEN WAITING | WAITING |
| AND I WANT TO | |

**WILL.** Michael. We'd never even spoken – he's football, prom king, maybe first runner-up but you know what I mean.

Then in this last week of school he just turns to me and starts...talking. To me. About, I don't even know! I wasn't listening because all I could think was I thought I was the only one like me in Nebraska, you know.

And then as school ends forever he says, "Maybe I'll see you around," and then he...

> *(Phone begins to ring but* **WILL** *ignores it.)*

Are you ready for this? ...he sang. He burst into song. "You are not so old." I thought: My life has finally become the musical I always suspected it was. Then he handed me this tape and said, "I made this for you. I thought you'd like it."

> *(***WILL*** *picks up the phone.)*

...Hold on.

> *(He answers the phone.)*

Hello and Happy New Year!

**MIKE.** Umm... Will?

**WILL.** Yes.

**MIKE.** It's Mike.

> *(***WILL*** *drops the phone – he scrambles to pick it up.)*

**WILL.** Oh, hey, hey, sorry. Hold on.

> (*He rushes to turn the music down, as he does, the* **BAND** *plays softer.*)

Hello?

**MIKE.** Hey, it's Mike. From Mr. Brown's class.

**WILL.** I heard you, sorry...just turning the...uh...

**MIKE.** You're listening to the tape I made you!

**WILL.** Yeah, yeah, yeah.

**MIKE.** It's good, right? Hey – Did you say Happy New Year?

**WILL.** No.

**MIKE.** Oh. I'm...uh...I'm going to the drive-in tonight. If you wanna go.

**WILL.** (*Speechless.*) Umm...

**MIKE.** You wanna go with me?

**WILL.** Umm...okay?

**MIKE.** Alright, cool. I'll pick you up at like eight, eight-thirty? I can hear your music – I love music. Hey! I'm listening to the same song!

> (**MICHAEL** *sings into the phone.*)

**MIKE & WILL.**

WHEN YOU SAID TO ME, "YOU ARE NOT SO OLD."
DID I KNOW IT THEN, 'CAUSE I HAD JUST BEEN TOLD

> (*They both sing into the phone.*)

| MIKE & WILL. | BACKUPS. |
|---|---|
| YOU KNOW I DIDN'T THINK | |
| I'D FIND YOU | |
| PERFECT IN SO MANY WAYS | |
| AND I'VE BEEN WAITING | WAITING |
| AND I WANT TO HAVE YOU | HAVE YOU |
| I'VE BEEN WAITING | WAITING |
| AND I WANT TO HAVE YOU | HAVE YOU |
| I'VE BEEN WAITING | WAITING |
| AND I WANT TO HAVE YOU | HAVE YOU |
| I'VE BEEN WAITING | WAITING |
| AND I WANT TO... | |

MIKE. *(Suddenly.)* K. Bye.

> (**MIKE** *hangs up.*)

> (**WILL** *looks at us in surprise.*)

WILL. What is happening? The drive-in? With a boy? This is the best New Year's ever!

> (**WILL** *jumps around and sings the end of the song.*)

| MIKE & WILL. | BACKUPS. |
|---|---|
| I'VE BEEN WAITING! | WAITING |
| I'VE BEEN WAITING! | WAITING |
| I'VE BEEN WAITING! | WAITING |
| I'VE BEEN WAITING! | WAITING |

> (*The song ends and the lights fade.*)

## Scene Two

*(When the lights come back up, **MIKE** and **WILL** are sitting side by side in Mike's car. [The car is simple – maybe just two chairs.] The two boys sit watching the movie at the drive-in. There is a long moment where **MIKE** is completely engrossed in the film and **WILL** is nervous and uncomfortable. **MIKE** turns his head slowly to look at **WILL**, then he looks back at the screen.)*

**WILL.** Wouldn't it be funny if they started singing? If they threw down their guns and... Isn't that the guy who was *shot* in the last scene? I don't... Comic book movies – Evangeline? I've never heard of...her. She's a nun but she's a superhero? It's good, it's just... *(New thought.)* I think my neighbor was a nun. I think she left the iron on or...something...this one time...because her house caught on fire in the middle of the night... What was she ironing? And why wasn't she home? Nuns don't... work. At night. Right? I never really understood that... event. I just remember the fire truck. Wait, why would a nun have a house? I don't think she was a nun.

**MIKE.** Do you always talk this much?

**WILL.** No.

*(There is a long, awkward silence. They watch the film.)*

**MIKE.** Do you like this movie?

**WILL.** Yeah. I do. It's a little violent, but...

**MIKE.** You sound like my girlfriend.

*(Silence.)*

**WILL.** You have a girlfriend?

**MIKE.** Kinda.

**WILL.** Oh, I didn't... I mean, I didn't...

**MIKE.** No, it's... She's... I don't even know...

**WILL.** You don't have to...

**MIKE.** I know. I don't have to what?

**WILL.** Explain.

**MIKE.** I know.

> *(Awkward pause.)*

She's gonna go to college in Chadron, and I'm gonna go to Lincoln, so we'll be like three hundred miles from each other, so...

> *(Pause. They watch the movie.)*

**WILL.** She's gorgeous.

**MIKE.** My girlfriend?

**WILL.** This woman, the...uh...Evangeline.

**MIKE.** Oh. Yeah. I was going to say, I didn't think you knew my girlfriend.

**WILL.** I don't – do I?

**MIKE.** You don't know her.

> *(Silence.)*

I like her arms.

**WILL.** Your girlfriend?

**MIKE.** Evangeline.

**WILL.** Oh.

**MIKE.** They're, like, long and thin. Like a spider. I like that, I like long, thin arms.

**WILL.** Hmmm.

> *(**WILL** surreptitiously looks at his own arms, which are long and thin. He smiles. They watch the film in silence. We hear the soundtrack of the film – people being shot. Screaming. Gun-fire, explosions. The "Love Theme" from the film begins to play, quietly.)*

Oh. There she goes. Ripping off her wimple with those long, thin arms – I should've seen it coming. Now he knows who she really is. *(Responding to the music.)* Oh, yeah – this is the...love theme...

*(We hear lines from the movie – it is* **EVANGELINE** *and the* **MAN** *who loves her.)*

**MAN.** *You're a mystery, you know that, right?*

**EVANGELINE.** *I'm not. I'm simple.*

**MAN.** *Not to me.*

**EVANGELINE.** *You'll see. I'm no more of a mystery than you.*

**WILL.** And...credits.

**MIKE.** Yep. Yeah – I guess I like strange things. You'd like my girlfriend – you remind me of her.

**WILL.** Huh. Is she in our class?

**MIKE.** Oh...no, no. She lives in another town, so...

**WILL.** Yeah.

**MIKE.** Yup. I guess it's over. The movie.

**WILL.** Yup.

> *(The music from "Winona" [the "Love Theme"] swells – it's the music over the credits.)*
>
> *(They speak the following two lines at the same time.)*

I hate the credits.

**MIKE.** I love the credits. Oh...

**WILL.** I mean, I don't...

**MIKE.** ...We can...

**WILL.** ...Hate...them...

**MIKE.** ...Go... I'll...yeah, yeah – you know – let's go. We can beat the... Let's go.

> *(The boys drive in awkward silence. Finally,* **MIKE** *speaks.)*

Did you – listen to the rest of the tape?

**WILL.** Twice.

**MIKE.** Cool. You like it?

**WILL.** Yeah.

MIKE. Yeah. I really like music. A lot...a lot a lot a lot, it's the only thing that keeps me from...

WILL. Oh, I know. Me, too.

MIKE. It keeps me...

> (WILL *looks out the window as they drive. He sees that* MIKE *is not making the turn he should make – He looks worried.*)

WILL. Oh – umm...sorry...you know...if you turn down Butte Avenue...it's... I'm like right...you know...it's faster –

MIKE. Oh – I know. I know. I just...wanted to avoid the Butte... Friday night. Everyone'll be out...so if it's okay we'll take the...other...

> (*Pause.*)

WILL. Do you and your girlfriend ever "cruise the Butte"?

MIKE. Oh, she doesn't like it. So, no. I mean, she says it's weird, driving up and down the main street, over and over again all night long doing what? Seeing who else is doing the exact same thing, only maybe in someone else's car this week, and who's riding in whose car, and who someone's girlfriend is, or whatever. It's stupid.

WILL. Yeah –

## Scene Three

*(They pull into Will's driveway.)*

**MIKE.** See – that didn't take much longer –

**WILL.** Thanks for the ride.

**MIKE.** Sure, it's no problem, since you were already in the car.

*(**WILL** doesn't get that **MIKE** is joking.)*

**WILL.** Alright, well...have a good night.

**MIKE.** Alright, man.

*(**WILL** can't find the door handle. He starts off trying to play it cool, but it becomes awkward and desperate. **MIKE** reaches across **WILL** and in an intimate and awkward moment, opens the door for him. **WILL** steps out.)*

*(Pause. **MIKE** looks as if he's going to say something, but doesn't.)*

**WILL.** I'll see ya.

**MIKE.** Alright, man.

*(**WILL** walks off as **MIKE** drives away. **WILL** looks up.)*

**WILL.** Stupid stars.

*(**MIKE** turns on his car-radio. **WILL** goes into his room, puts his headphones on, and presses play on the tape player. He and **MIKE** are listening to the same song.)*

### [MUSIC NO. 03 "REACHING OUT"]

YOU'VE COUNTED EVERY STAR
THAT YOU COULD IMAGINE
BROKEN WHEN EVERYONE TOOK YOU FOR A FOOL
IT GAVE YOU A REASON
TO FIND SOMETHING STRONG ENOUGH TO FEEL

YOU'RE REACHING OUT, REACHING OUT

REACHING OUT, REACHING OUT
REACHING OUT.

> (**MIKE** *pulls over, gets out of his car, grabs a guitar out of the back, and starts playing along.*)

**MIKE.** I'm an idiot. My dad laid into me earlier. About my grades, of course – I said, "Dad! Guess what? High school is over! I already got a full-ride to the University." He said, "One day you'll wish you could say you were Valedictorian and you'll feel like a fool because you weren't. People remember those things." He's good at making me feel like an idiot, and *now*...

> (*He plays a fancy guitar solo.*)

Taught myself how to play. Drive out to the country, park my car, sit on the hood, play, look at the stars. Will's cool. Spider-arms? Man, maybe my dad's right – I am a fool.

**MIKE & WILL.**

I'VE COUNTED EVERY STAR
THAT YOU COULD IMAGINE
BROKEN WHEN EVERYONE TOOK ME FOR A FOOL
IT GAVE ME A REASON
TO FIND SOMETHING STRONG ENOUGH TO FEEL

**WILL.**

YOU'RE REACHING OUT,

**MIKE & WILL.**

REACHING OUT

**WILL.**

REACHING OUT,

**MIKE & WILL.**

REACHING OUT
YOU'RE REACHING OUT

> (**MIKE** *goes into this bedroom and lies on his bed – he and* **WILL** *are mirroring each other – lying on their beds listening to the same song.*)

AND IF I CAN'T KNOW YOU
ALL MY DREAMS ARE THROUGH
EVERY WAKING HOUR IS FILLED WITH LEAD
I'M DEAD, I'M DEAD.

*(Music ends.)*

*(Both boys lie on their beds in silence, staring
at the ceiling. The lights fade on them.)*

## Scene Four

> *(Lights come up. It is the next morning –
> neither boy has moved.* **MIKE** *picks up his
> phone and dials. Will's phone rings.)*

**WILL.** Hello?

**MIKE.** Hello, Will?

**WILL.** Yes?

**MIKE.** Hi, it's Mike.

**WILL.** Oh. Hi.

> *(Pause.)*

Hello?

**MIKE.** Hello.

**WILL.** Oh, I thought you'd hung up.

**MIKE.** Nope, I'm here.

**WILL.** Oh.

**MIKE.** So, did you like the movie last night?

**WILL.** Yeah.

> *(Pause.)*

I like the way the surprises kept unfolding. Oh, look,
she's a nun. Oh, no, she's actually a cop. No, she's a
superhero. No, forget it, forget it, she's an *alien.*
An Alien-Nun.

**MIKE.** You're funny.

**WILL.** No I'm not.

**MIKE.** Do you...want to go again tonight?

**WILL.** To the movie?

**MIKE.** Uh-huh.

**WILL.** Umm... Okay. What's it gonna be?

**MIKE.** I guess it's... I don't know, just two friends hanging
out.

**WILL.** I mean what is the movie?

**MIKE.** Oh. I know. The movie, it's...the same one, the same
movie we saw last night.

**WILL.** You want to see *Evangeline* again?

**MIKE.** You like it, right?

**WILL.** Yes.

**MIKE.** So, you want to?

**WILL.** Tonight?

**MIKE.** Yeah.

**WILL.** Yeah.

**MIKE.** Yeah?

**WILL.** Yeah.

**MIKE.** Okay.

**WILL.** Okay.

**MIKE.** Should I just pick you up?

**WILL.** Uh-huh.

**MIKE.** Okay.

**WILL.** Okay.

**MIKE.** Will?

**WILL.** Yeah?

    *(Pause.)*

**MIKE.** Nothing.

**WILL.** Okay.

    *(They both hang up. **MIKE** slaps his forehead
    and shakes his head. **WILL** looks at us.)*

  Yay!

    *(Lights go black.)*

## Scene Five

*(When the lights come back up, we are at the movie again. They are sitting in uncomfortable silence once again. We hear the same sound effects.)*

**WILL.** I didn't notice the first time that she used that crucifix for so many things.

*(**MIKE** says nothing. **WILL** is less interested in the film this time – he looks around at the other cars.)*

Aren't those your friends over there?

**MIKE.** Where?

**WILL.** Over there.

**MIKE.** Oh, man, yeah. Shit.

**WILL.** What's wrong?

**MIKE.** Oh, nothing, I just didn't know they'd be here. Could you just, like, like duck down a little? No, no, nevermind, no that's stupid, don't do that, nevermind.

*(Silence.)*

Oh, no, don't come over here. Ummm...hold on... I'm gonna just go talk to them for a minute so they don't come over here. Just sit here, okay?

*(He goes. **WILL** watches him go, then sits in long silence. Then looks at us.)*

**WILL.** David Harris. Andy Cooke. And *Justin Mently.*
David Harris is the one fat kid who gets to be popular.
And he's always wearing a wrestling...whatdoyoucallit.
Leotard.
Andy Cooke is like twenty-five. I think he buys beer for everyone.
Justin Mentley. *(Seething.)* Mentley. He walks around at *all* times with a baseball bat on his shoulder...like... is he always playing baseball...? Or, like, is that just his...'cause he's...like... I feel like he's probably killed

someone. I mean not actually, but... *(Sigh.)* He's got really sexy arms, though. Oh, God.

> *(**WILL** watches the movie. He surreptitiously looks out the window to **MIKE**, then back to the movie. After a moment, **MIKE** comes back, gets into the car.)*

**MIKE.** Hey.

**WILL.** What'd they want?

**MIKE.** Oh, I don't know. They're playing this baseball tournament in a few weeks. It's a summer...thing... They were wondering if I was gonna do it.

**WILL.** Oh.

**MIKE.** Yeah, I told them I would. It's fun, I guess. We do it every year, it's just a bunch of guys on teams.

> *(Pause.)*

I told them I was with my girlfriend.

> *(**WILL** looks to the backseat – as if looking for the girlfriend. **MIKE** laughs.)*

**WILL.** She lives far away?

**MIKE.** Hemingford.

**WILL.** Oh, so just a quick little... Not bad.

> *(Pause. **MIKE** is still nervous about the friends.)*

**MIKE.** I don't know why they're here, together like that. They don't even like movies. They usually come just to make-out with their girlfriends.

**WILL.** It is a drive-in. You don't...make-out?

**MIKE.** Watch this part.

> *(They watch.)*

**WILL.** Have you had sex with her?

**MIKE.** Jesus!

**WILL.** What?

**MIKE.** Why are you asking me all this stuff?

**WILL.** I don't know, isn't this what guys talk about?

**MIKE.** You're a guy. You know...you know...things...you... know... Why don't you have a girlfriend?

(*Pause.*)

**WILL.** I don't know.

**MIKE.** Have you ever had one?

**WILL.** No.

**MIKE.** Do you...ever...want a...girlfriend?

**WILL.** Why are you asking me all this stuff?

**MIKE.** I don't know, isn't this what guys talk about?

**WILL.** You're a guy.

**MIKE.** I know.

**WILL.** I've had...crushes on...before. But...nothing...

**MIKE.** Who?

**WILL.** I'm not telling you.

**MIKE.** Come on! I promise I won't laugh.

(*Silence.*)

So you've never...?

(**WILL** *has clammed up.*)

And...people at school say...things to you?

**WILL.** Or pin me down and write a certain word across my forehead with permanent marker.

(*Silence.*)

**MIKE.** Can I confess something?

**WILL.** Oh my god.

**MIKE.** What?

**WILL.** Nothing.

**MIKE.** My girlfriend... She knows what she wants, I mean, that's what I meant before, why you remind me of her. And I don't. I wish I knew.

**WILL.** I thought you wanted to be a doctor. A brain surgeon, what was it?

**MIKE.** Yeah, maybe, I don't know

**WILL.** Do what you want to do.

(**MIKE** *sings quietly to himself from "I Wanted To Tell You".*)

**MIKE.**

DO JUST WHAT YOU WANT TO.

(*They watch the movie for a second.*)

I don't even know what a "brain surgeon" is, really, I mean, besides the obvious. It's like saying you want to be a pirate. I like music. "Do just what you want to," you should hear me play that one. It's just because my dad's a doctor. Man, if he ever heard me say that! What are *you* gonna be?

(*Pause.* **WILL** *looks at the screen.*)

**WILL.** A nun. No, a cop. No, a superhero. No, forget it. An alien. An Alien-Nun.

**MIKE.** Why do you talk like that?

**WILL.** Like what?

**MIKE.** So obvious. (*Starts.*) Should we go?

**WILL.** Why?

**MIKE.** Here comes the end of the movie, and I know you don't like the credits...

**WILL.** Oh. No, no – I want to watch them.

**MIKE.** You do?

**WILL.** Yeah – I want to... I like that song... I think you'd be a good brain surgeon if that's what you wanted to be.

(**MIKE** *settles back in.*)

**MIKE.** I want to confess something else. But don't look at me, okay? And...don't talk...just pretend you're watching the movie.

(**WILL** *does.*)

I only ever come to the movies alone. I'm always alone. On purpose; I don't like... But I like hanging out with you. And it's supposed to be your friend... I mean, I think about things. Like that.

(**MIKE** *turns up the volume.*)

**MIKE.** How something...could be perfect if...you weren't *you*...

It's just...like... You know?

### [MUSIC NO. 04 "WINONA"]

Perfect. Do you know what I'm saying?

**WILL.** I *think* so.

**MIKE.** Yeah. Like...like this movie – this guy here, you know, he wants to find this girl, and he hasn't got her figured out, but he wants to. And then, you know, she's been right there the whole time, it's just that she wasn't who he thought. My girlfriend...is not...

I TRIED TO CALL YOU BUT THE LINE WAS BUSY
WERE YOU TALKING TO A FRIEND?
AND WHEN I TRIED AGAIN MUCH LATER
I DIDN'T WANT TO LET IT RING AGAIN.
SO YOU SEE I'VE GOT A PROBLEM
BACK BY POPULAR DEMAND
SOMETIMES I WANT TO KEEP IT FROM YOU
SOMETIMES I THINK YOU'LL UNDERSTAND
COULD YOU BE MY LITTLE MOVIE STAR?

**MIKE & BACKUPS.**

COULD YOU BE MY LONG LOST GIRL?
IT'S TRUE THAT I DON'T REALLY KNOW YOU
BUT I'M ALONE IN THE WORLD.

*(We hear lines from the movie – It is* **EVANGELINE** *and the* **MAN** *who loves her.)*

**MAN.** *You're a mystery, you know that, right?*

**EVANGELINE.** *I'm not. I'm simple.*

**MAN.** *Not to me.*

**EVANGELINE.** *You'll see. I'm no more of a mystery than you.*

**MIKE.**

AND WHEN I THINK MAYBE I NEED YOU
I DON'T CARE IF IT'S NOT TRUE
BECAUSE IT ISN'T SO MUCH WHAT I NEED NOW

**MIKE & BACKUPS.**

AS WHAT I WANT FROM YOU

**MIKE.**

COULD YOU BE MY LITTLE MOVIE STAR?

**MIKE & BACKUPS.**

COULD YOU BE MY LONG LOST GIRL?

IT'S TRUE THAT I DON'T REALLY KNOW YOU

BUT I'M ALONE IN THE WORLD

**MIKE.**

COULD YOU BE MY LITTLE MOVIE STAR?

**MIKE & BACKUPS.**

COULD YOU BE MY LONG LOST GIRL?

IT'S TRUE THAT I DON'T REALLY KNOW YOU

I FEEL ALONE

I FEEL ALONE

> *(The music continues and the lights shift as* **WILL** *walks downstage to us.)*

**WILL.** Every night for two weeks, when Michael and I sit here, watching this same movie and it gets to the credits, with the love theme, he sings, and I think of these imaginary people on the other side of the screen watching us and saying to themselves, "Oh, my! *This* is romantic."

> *(There is a magical little moment where* **WILL** *stays suspended outside the scene.)*
>
> *(Music ends.)*
>
> *(The lights shift to...)*

## Scene Six

*(...**WILL** on his front step. He speaks to us.)*

**WILL.** It's so warm this summer. I wish I were swimming in some steamy sea with Michael. I already feel like I'm in *Grease* – the movie, not the country. Summer nights. The Drive-in. A sports car. Well, a Subaru.

> *(**WILL** sits, waiting – as if he's expecting someone. He begins rhythmically playing his thighs like drums. After a moment, he stops.)*

Waiting.

*(Sung from "I've Been Waiting".)* WAITING.

He asked me if I would Run Errands with him. *Run Errands.* I've been waiting my whole life for a boy to ask me to run errands with him. I hope we have to pick up dog food. Walking through Safeway with Michael pushing a shopping cart with a big bag of dog food... Uh! When did my life become like my dreams?

> *(**MIKE** appears.)*

Hey.

**MIKE.** Hi. You ready?

**WILL.** Yup. Where are we going?

**MIKE.** I need to go to Safeway.

**WILL.** *(Gasp.)* Really?

**MIKE.** I need to pick something up.

**WILL.** *(More excited.)* Really?

**MIKE.** Yeah, I need your help.

**WILL.** *(Too excited.)* 'Cause it's so big and hard to carry?

**MIKE.** Yeah.

**WILL.** *(Over-the-top.)* Is it dog food?!

**MIKE.** No. Boxes.

**WILL.** *(Disappointed.)* Oh.

**MIKE.** My dad's on a tear – I swear he has spies that follow me around and report back to him about who

I'm hanging out with or... I need to... I'm gonna start packing my stuff up. So – boxes.

*(They walk in silence.)*

*(Singing quietly, from "Looking At The Sun".)*
DO YOU REALLY WANT TO RUN AWAY WITH ME?

*(**MIKE** notices that **WILL** is staring at him.)*

**WILL.** I like it when you sing.

**MIKE.** Making fun.

**WILL.** No! I like that one. How's it go?

**MIKE.**
DO YOU REALLY WANT TO RUN AWAY WITH ME?
*(Stops singing.)* Where are you gonna go?

**WILL.** What?

**MIKE.** I mean, after the summer's over now that high school... I mean you're not going to *college*, right, so...?

**WILL.** Oh. *(Laughs.)* Yeah. I don't know.

**MIKE.** Oh.

**WILL.** What?

**MIKE.** Thought maybe you had some big, exciting plan – Europe or... I don't know. Something...

**WILL.** Europe? No. Do people do that?

**MIKE.** I don't know, yeah. People, I guess...

**WILL.** What would I do there?

**MIKE.** What would you do here?

**WILL.** I don't know, my *mom* and like money and stuff.

**MIKE.** You should get out of here.

**WILL.** *(Changing the subject.)* Sing that song.

**MIKE.** No!

### [MUSIC NO. 05 "LOOKING AT THE SUN"]

**WILL.** Come on!

**MIKE.** No!

**WILL.** Chicken.

**MIKE.** Oh, like that's gonna work.

*(Silence. **WILL** clucks like a chicken.)*

*(**MIKE** gives in and sings.)*

**MIKE.**

DO YOU REALLY WANT TO RUN AWAY WITH ME?
WOULD YOU REALLY LIKE TO RUN AWAY WITH ME?
I CAN FEEL VERY CLEARLY BUT NO LONGER SEE.

| **MIKE.** | **BACKUPS.** |
|---|---|
| FOR, OH! LOOKING AT THE SUN | AHH |
| WAITING FOR YOU TO APPEAR | |
| WATCHED YOU GETTING NEARER | AHHH |

**MIKE.**

LIKE I KNEW IT IN MY HEART
THE DAMAGE WAS ALREADY DONE
LOOKING AT THE SUN
BURNED MY EYES OUT
AND I'M BLIND NOW.

**WILL.** That was good. You're not a chicken. Put a little soul into it.

*(**MIKE** does a little "soul" dance on the next lyric – it's awkward.)*

**MIKE.**

I WAS LOOKING FOR SOMEBODY THAT YOU COULDN'T BE

**WILL.** *(Laughing)* Okay – no soul.

**MIKE.**

I WAS LOOKING FOR SOMEBODY YOU WOULD NEVER BE.
I WAS SO SURE THAT THERE WAS NOTHING WRONG WITH ME!

**WILL.** Wow! That Was Amazing.

*(They sing ecstatically and in perfect harmony.)*

| **MIKE & WILL.** | **BACKUPS.** |
|---|---|
| OH! LOOKING AT THE SUN | AHH |
| WAITING FOR YOU TO APPEAR | |
| WATCHED YOU GETTING NEARER | AHH |

**MIKE & WILL.**

LIKE I KNEW IT IN MY HEART

THE DAMAGE WAS ALREADY DONE
LOOKING AT THE SUN
BURNED MY EYES OUT
AND I'M BLIND NOW
I'M BLIND!

> *(Guitar solo.)*

DO YOU REALLY WANNA RUN AWAY WITH ME?
I CAN FEEL VERY CLEARLY, BUT NO LONGER...

**MIKE & WILL.**                              **BACKUPS.**

| | |
|---|---|
| OH! LOOKING AT THE SUN | AHH |
| WAITING FOR YOU TO APPEAR | |
| WATCHED YOU GETTING NEARER | AHH |
| LIKE I KNEW IT IN MY HEART | |
| THE DAMAGE WAS ALREADY DONE | |
| LOOKING AT THE SUN BURNED MY EYES OUT, | |
| NOW I'M BLIND! | AHH |
| LOOKING AT THE SUN | AHH |
| WAITING FOR YOU TO APPEAR | |
| WATCHED YOU GETTING NEARER | AHH |

**MIKE & WILL.**

LIKE I KNEW IT IN MY HEART
THE DAMAGE WAS ALREADY DONE
LOOKING AT THE SUN
BURNED MY EYES OUT,
AND I'M BLIND NOW
AND, I'M BLIND NOW.

> *(Music ends.)*

> *(They are happy – it's a perfect day.)*

**WILL.** Don't you love the way summer smells? Even these
ugly buildings – kinda pretty with that smell –

> *(They're suddenly very close to each other,
> but don't notice it until they hear a car speed
> away as someone yells, "Faggots!" The boys
> jump away from each other.)*

*(Awkward silence. A loud train passes.)*

*(They both try to pretend nothing just happened.)*

**MIKE.** I hate this place

**WILL.** The things people... I mean...it doesn't *matter*... I wouldn't... Be... I mean, I'm not... You don't have to run away because of what people say.

**MIKE.** I've got baseball practice at five o'clock. Then my girlfriend's coming over to help me pack. I'm leaving early – to Lincoln. Like, in a week, so, boxes.

> **(MICHAEL** *hurries on ahead.* **WILL** *stands still and looks at us.)*

**WILL.** *(Sincerely.)* Stop looking at me like that.

> *(Lights fade.)*

## Scene Seven

*(Later that night.* **MIKE** *enters his bedroom. He is very upset. He slams the door.)*

*(***MIKE*** *picks up the phone and dials.)*

*(Lights shift.* **WILL** *is home. The phone rings.)*

**WILL.** Hello?

**MIKE.** *(Yelling, so his father can hear.)* Hey, Baby! It's MIKE!

**WILL.** Hello?

**MIKE.** *(Still yelling.)* How 'bout I come pick you up? *(Yelling to his father.)* HAPPY?!

**WILL.** Why are you screaming at me?

**MIKE.** *(Now quietly, just to* **WILL.***)* Not you. I'm just pissed off – God. My fucking dad! He's so interested in my fucking girlfriend he should take her out.
"What are your plans for tonight, son?"
"Nothing, Dad."
"Well, I thought you had plans with your young lady?"
"Yeah, well, I changed my mind."
"Why, so you can go hang out with your friend?"
*(Getting furious.)* FUCK!
*(New thought.)* What are you doing?

**WILL.** Nothing.

**MIKE.** I'm going to come pick you up, okay?

**WILL.** Maybe I have plans.

**MIKE.** You don't have plans.

**WILL.** I might.

**MIKE.** Do you?

**WILL.** No.

**MIKE.** I'll be there in a minute.

**WILL.** I don't know.

**MIKE.** Come on.

*(Silence.)*

**MIKE.** I'm... I...didn't mean...earlier...to...

**WILL.** It's okay.

**MIKE.** Can I come pick you up?

**WILL.** What are we gonna do?

**MIKE.** I don't know.

**WILL.** Okay. *Baby*.

> *(Lights shift.)*

## Scene Eight

*(The boys are in the car.)*

**[MUSIC NO. 6 "GIRLFRIEND"]**

*(This is the actual recording of the song, playing on the radio.)*

*(Driving fast. MIKE is silent and fuming. Tension.)*

*(WILL turns the radio up, MIKE is annoyed.)*

**MIKE.** It's a little loud.

**WILL.** It's not loud, it's rock and roll. *(He turns it up louder.)* Come on, you love this song. Forget about your dad! Oh, man! I love this song!! It's rock and roll. Who cares? Rock and Roll!

> *(The music stays loud, they drive and listen, kind of singing along. WILL is acting goofy to get MIKE to smile.)*

**RADIO.** *(Recorded.)*

I WANNA LOVE SOMEBODY.

**WILL.** This is my favorite one, definitely.

**RADIO.** *(Recorded.)*

I HEAR YOU NEED SOMEBODY TO LOVE.
I WANNA LOVE SOMEBODY.

**WILL.** Let's roll the windows down.

**RADIO.** *(Recorded.)*

I HEAR YOU'RE LOOKING FOR SOMEONE TO LOVE
'CAUSE YOU NEED TO GET BACK IN THE ARMS
OF A GOOD FRIEND
AND I NEED TO GET BACK IN THE ARMS OF A GIRLFRIEND.

> *(A pause in the music – silence. They look at each other. A big smile, a big breath, and as they sing the next lyric, the BAND takes over for the recording – this is suddenly live. The boys are ecstatically singing.)*

**MIKE & WILL.**

> I DIDN'T KNOW NOBODY
> AND THEN I SAW YOU COMIN' MY WAY
> I DIDN'T KNOW NOBODY
> AND THEN I SAW YOU COMIN' MY WAY
> DON'T YOU NEED TO

**BACKUPS.**

> AHH
> AHH
> AHH
> AHH

**MIKE & WILL.**

> GET BACK IN THE ARMS
> OF A GOOD FRIEND?
> OH, 'CAUSE HONEY BELIEVE ME,

**BACKUPS.**

> AHH
> AHH
> AHH
> AHH

**MIKE & WILL.**

> I'D SURE LOVE TO CALL YOU
> MY GIRLFRIEND. OOH!

> > (**MIKE** *puts his arm out the window.* **WILL** *does the same. They can barely hear each other, the music is so loud – they're shouting now!)*

**WILL.** Ooh, look: that old barn always freaks me out – did you know a Satanic Cult used to live there? Go down this road behind it. Here.

**MIKE.** Where?

**WILL.** Here. Here. This road.

**MIKE.** There was never a cult. That's a kids' story. Where are we?

**WILL.** There *was*... I don't know – oh, wow, look... You're telling me that's not a Satanic Cult-looking barn? Honk as we pass it – HONK!

> > (**MIKE** *honks the car horn, the tires squeal, the boys laugh.)*

Go! *FUCK YOU SATAN!*

| WILL. | BACKUPS. |
|---|---|
| DON'T YOU NEED TO GET BACK | AHH AHH |
|  | AHH AHH |

IN THE ARMS OF A GOOD FRIEND?

**MIKE.**

OH, 'CAUSE HONEY BELIEVE ME                    AHH AHH

AHH AHH

I'D SURE LOVE TO CALL YOU MY
    GIRLFRIEND.

**WILL.**

'CAUSE YOU GOT A GOOD THING GOING, BABY

**MIKE & WILL.**

YOU ONLY NEED SOMEBODY TO LOVE

**MIKE.**

YOU GOT A GOOD THING GOING

**MIKE & WILL.**

YOU'RE ONLY LOOKING FOR SOMEONE TO LOVE
'CAUSE YOU NEED TO

**BACKUPS.**

    AHH

    AHH

    AHH

    AHH

**MIKE & WILL.**

GET BACK IN THE ARMS OF A GOOD FRIEND.

*(They look at each other, completely uninhibited.)*

**WILL.** Drum Solo!

*(**MIKE** does a ridiculous drum solo on the dash. **WILL** plays the air-bass.)*

| MIKE & WILL. | BACKUPS. |
|---|---|
| AND I'M NEVER GONNA SET YOU FREE! | AHH AHH |
| NO I'M NEVER GONNA SET YOU FREE! | AHH |

*(Music ends.)*

## Scene Nine

> *(They've stopped the car in the middle of a field.)*

**WILL.** How does it get so dark out here? You'd think all of those stars... It's like we're just out there, isn't it, in outer space? It feels like that.

**MIKE.** I used to always wish the sun wouldn't come back up.

**WILL.** My dad moved to Utah.

**MIKE.** They're divorced?

**WILL.** Yup.

> *(They are sitting on the hood of the car.)*

**MIKE.** That's cool. I didn't mean to tell you like that. Before. That I'm going to school early – I am – like in a week, or something. I think you can start classes, pre-med, or whatever, I *TOLD* my dad I could start classes early – just so I can get the hell out of *HIS HOUSE*! I can't wait to be gone. Why do you smell like smoke?

**WILL.** Sorry. It's my mom. I've smelled like this all my life.

**MIKE.** I've never noticed it till right now.

**WILL.** Really?

**MIKE.** Really.

**WILL.** I've been embarrassed about it since kindergarten. I usually wash my clothes before I go anywhere – didn't have time tonight. I used to steal clothes from my cousins and put them in my desk at school so I could change into them. Once I grabbed my cousin Jennifer's shirt by mistake. So all day I was "Daddy's Little Princess." I tried to play it off as ironic, but, third-graders. You know.

> *(**MIKE** laughs a little.)*

What? *What?*

> *(**MIKE** laughs more.)*

**MIKE.** "Daddy's Little Princess."

**WILL.** It's not that funny.

> (**MIKE** *laughs harder.*)

It was embarrassing. It *is* embarrassing.

> (*The laughter dies out. They look at each other.*)

What?

**MIKE.** Nothing. *(Beat.)* You think I'm...what, handsome, or whatever?

**WILL.** Ummm... *(Scared to answer.)*

**MIKE.** I'm not making fun of you.

**WILL.** Oh.

**MIKE.** So do you?

**WILL.** Ummm...yeah.

**MIKE.** Hmm. I wish... Maybe you are handsome. Maybe I could think that. I don't know, let me look at you.

**WILL.** It's so dark.

**MIKE.** I know.

**WILL.** Well, here.

> (*He takes* **MIKE**'s *hand and puts it on his face.* **MIKE** *plays along.*)

**MIKE.** Hmm. Yes, you're...handsome. Nice. Funny. Cool. I like that.

> (*Pause.* **MIKE** *keeps his hands on* **WILL**'s *face a moment too long. Then lets them down.*)

I guess I'll miss this place a little.

**WILL.** You sound like you might as well be going to the moon.

**MIKE.** Yeah, well. The moon's alright, I guess. I'm sorry about your dad.

**WILL.** Eh.

**MIKE.** Dads suck. Mine's going out of town for the weekend, thank God. I'm packing up my stuff so when he comes home I'm gone.

**WILL.** I thought a week?

(**MIKE** *grabs his guitar.*)

**MIKE.** This is what I usually do out here.

(*He begins to play the guitar.*)

### [MUSIC NO. 07 "WE'RE THE SAME"]

(*Just* **MIKE** *on guitar.*)

**WILL.** How was baseball practice?

**MIKE.** Fine.

**WILL.** How was your girlfriend?

(*No response.*)

**MIKE.**

    I DON'T HAVE TO SPEAK
    AND YOU KNOW WHAT I'M THINKING
    YOU DON'T NEED TO HEAR WHAT I SAY
    I DON'T HAVE TO ASK 'CAUSE YOU'LL GUESS
    WHAT I'M SEEKING
    YOU DON'T NEED TO HIDE
    WHAT YOU KNOW.

**MIKE & WILL.** (**WILL** *sings "babys" and humming.*)

    BABY, WE'RE THE SAME
    WHEN WE FAIL IN EACH OTHER'S EYES
    BABY, WE'RE THE SAME

**MIKE & WILL.**

    SO YOU SHOULD NOT BE SURPRISED
    WHEN I SWEAR TO YOU

**MIKE.**

    I NEVER TOLD YOU WHAT TO DO
    MAYBE IT'S ME MAYBE IT'S YOU.

(**MIKE** *keeps strumming chords.*)

**WILL.** You're good.

**MIKE.** Thanks.

**WILL.** I can play "Skidamarink a dink a dink" on the piano.

**MIKE.** I broke up with her.

**WILL.** Tonight?

**MIKE.** I told her I like someone else. You coming to my game tomorrow night?

**WILL.** Yeah.

**MIKE.** Good.

**WILL.** Don't go to the moon.

**MIKE.**

I DON'T HAVE TO ACT
SO YOU'LL KNOW WHAT I'M FEELING
YOU DON'T NEED TO SEE TO BELIEVE

**MIKE & WILL.** (**WILL** *sings "babys" and humming.*)

BABY, WE'RE THE SAME
WHEN WE SHINE IN EACH OTHER'S SKY
BABY, WE'RE THE SAME

**MIKE & WILL.**

SO YOU SHOULD NOT BE SURPRISED
WHEN I SWEAR TO YOU
I NEVER TOLD YOU WHAT TO DO

**MIKE.**

SOMETIMES IT'S ME
SOMETIMES IT'S YOU

(**WILL** *closes his eyes.* **MIKE** *stops playing.*)

Why are you closing your eyes?

(**WILL** *shrugs.* **MIKE** *stares at him.* **MIKE** *slowly leans in to kiss* **WILL** *– right as he gets close to* **WILL**'s *face,* **WILL** *opens his eyes and, being startled, jumps back and begins laughing. As soon as* **WILL** *stops laughing there is a moment of stillness – they look at each other and slowly, delicately kiss and then pull apart. The full* **BAND** *enters to finish the song.*)

| MIKE & WILL. | BACKUPS. |
|---|---|
| BABY, WE'RE THE SAME | BABY, WE'RE THE SAME |
| WHEN WE FAIL IN EACH OTHER'S EYES | OOH |
| BABY, WE'RE THE SAME | BABY, WE'RE THE SAME |

| MIKE & WILL. | BACKUPS. |
| --- | --- |
| SO YOU SHOULD NOT BE SURPRISED | OHH |
| WHEN I SWEAR TO YOU | |
| I NEVER TOLD YOU WHAT TO DO | I NEVER TOLD YOU WHAT TO DO |
| MAYBE IT'S ME | |
| MAYBE IT'S YOU | OHH |
| MAYBE IT'S YOU | OHH |
| | OHH |
| | OHH |
| | OHH |
| | OHH |

*(They lie back, side by side. MIKE shows WILL his hand – WILL looks at it and MIKE strangely. MIKE nods. WILL grabs his hand. They smile as the lights fade.)*

*(Immediately to...)*

# ACT II

## Scene One

*(Suddenly we hear the crack of a baseball bat hitting a ball – a homerun! A huge cheer from a crowd! An organ playing the classic baseball game wind-up.)*

*(We see **WILL** jumping up and down, cheering.)*

**WILL.** *(To us.)* I have no idea what's happening but I'm having the *best* time.

*(The crowd cheers. So does **WILL**.)*

*(Cheering.)* Yay! Baseball!

*(**MIKE** approaches, in his baseball clothes.)*

**MIKE.** Hey.

**WILL.** Hi! This is fun! I love baseball!

**MIKE.** The game's over.

**WILL.** Oh.

*(**MIKE** keeps turning back to see who's watching.)*

You played great.

**MIKE.** We lost.

**WILL.** You did? I didn't notice.

**MIKE.** We play tomorrow to see who gets last place. Stupid. Mently wants the team to go get pizza. It's kinda the last time I'll see these guys for a while, and they *are* my friends, or *were*, or... I should probably go with them...

Wanna go? Wait, no, nevermind. No, come, *yeah*, come...you know what – I'm not gonna go. Forget it.

**WILL.** Well, I think *I'm* going now, so...

(**MIKE** *laughs.*)

**MIKE.** I didn't sleep very well last night. *(Smiles.)* It's okay, though. I'm not tired. At all. I feel really good. I do stink, however. I should go change.

(**WILL** *smiles.*)

**WILL.** I feel really good, too. You smell like grass.

**MIKE.** Hmm.

**WILL.** I didn't sleep, either.

**MIKE.** Hmm.

**WILL.** *(Re: the boys.)* They're watching us.

**MIKE.** Hmm.

(**MIKE** *looks at the boys, then back to* **WILL.**)

What if I just kissed you right now?

(**MIKE** *laughs, a little nervously.*)

Can you imagine? I have an idea. Why don't we just go right now? I don't need to change, since I smell so good, apparently.

**WILL.** Hmm.

(*They stare at each other.*)

**MIKE.** Let's go. I thought I'd take you to my favorite place in the world.

## Scene Two

*(The lights shift. Once again, we're at the Drive-in. The same sound effects can be heard.)*

*(**MIKE** looks completely engrossed in the film.)*

*(**WILL** is bored with the movie and is rolling his eyes. He looks at **MIKE**.)*

**WILL.** Why would they show the same movie all summer?

**MIKE.** It's good.

**WILL.** I have to – can I tell you something? This... This is a terrible movie! We've got to find something else to do.

**MIKE.** I thought you liked it.

> *(**WILL** shakes his head. A sexy groove starts playing on the soundtrack [the **BAND**]).*

## [MUSIC NO. 08 "EVANGELINE"]

**WILL.** Like this – what's happening here?

**MIKE.** She's gotta trick this reporter into believing she's not who he thinks she is.

**WILL.** So she takes off her crime fighting leather bustier and semi-automatic crucifix to seduce this reporter so he won't discover her true identity – a nun.

**MIKE.** Right.

**WILL.** So the nun strips.

**MIKE.** Right.

**WILL.** That's a messed-up story. You love it!

**MIKE.** Yeah. It's good.

**WILL.** And then this music... They should just start singing.

**MIKE.** They're naked!

**WILL.** So... Let's make up our own...

> *(**WILL** is making up the words as he goes along. This is apparent.)*

**WILL.**

> SHE'S ON ANOTHER PLANET, SHE'S IN MY DREAM
> SHE'S SOME KIND OF ANGEL, IF YOU KNOW WHAT I MEAN
> TRY HER ON, AND SHE FITS LIKE A GLOVE
> TOO BAD SHE ONLY THINKS ABOUT THE LORD ABOVE
>
> EVANGELINE, EVANGELINE
> I THINK I LOVE YOU                    **BACKUPS.**
> EVANGELINE, EVANGELINE                EVANGELINE
> I WANT YOU

**MIKE.** That was pretty good.

**WILL.** Your turn. Go! You go, you go! You're the lead character. What do you sing to her when the camera is close up on your face? And you're naked.

> (**MIKE** *is taken off-guard – he starts singing.*)

**MIKE.**

> NOW IF I CALLED YOU UP DO YOU THINK
> YOU COULD DELIVER MY SOUL?
> WON'T YOU TAKE A DRINK LITTLE DARLING
> THE CUP IS FULL.                      **BACKUPS.**
> AND EVERY NIGHT I BOW TO PRAY          AHH
> BUT I'LL FEEL A WHOLE LOT BETTER
> ONCE YOU'RE COMING MY WAY              AHH

**WILL.** Nice!

**MIKE & WILL.**

> EVANGELINE, EVANGELINE
> I THINK I LOVE YOU                    **BACKUPS.**
> EVANGELINE, EVANGELINE                EVANGELINE
> I WANT YOU, SO COME ON DOWN.

**MIKE.** He seduces her. She's hesitant, but he eventually wins. He's kissed her once, and it changed everything. She can't deny her true feelings, you know? Forget this nun-nonsense.

**WILL.** (*As Evangeline, the nun.*)

> SO TELL ME HOW YOU WANT IT
> COME ON!

**MIKE.** *(As the action hero.)*          **BACKUPS.**

TELL ME HOW YOU WANT IT.              OOH, YEAH!

**WILL.**

*(As himself.)*

SO TELL ME HOW YOU WANT IT

WE WON'T BE SEEN

YOU CAN TELL YOUR FATHER IT WAS ALL A DREAM

**BACKUPS.**

*TRY HER ON, SHE FITS LIKE A GLOVE*

*(They get closer and closer until they are face to face.)*

**MIKE & WILL.**

EVANGELINE, EVANGELINE

I THINK I LOVE YOU

EVANGELINE, EVANGELINE

I WANT YOU!

*(Music ends.)*

*(**MIKE** kisses **WILL** – a deeper kiss this time, not as innocent. They are face to face.)*

**MIKE.** Let's go.

## Scene Three

*(The lights shift and we see the boys at Mike's house, in Mike's room.* **WILL** *sits on Mike's bed, looking around.* **MIKE** *surreptitiously slabs on some deodorant. He sits next to* **WILL**.*)*

*(Finally...)*

*(***MIKE*** *produces some Boone's Farm. They drink a little – straight from the bottle.)*

**MIKE.** What?

**WILL.** I didn't say anything.

**MIKE.** I thought you were going to.

**WILL.** Oh. No.

**MIKE.** Oh.

>  *(Pause.)*

Will you?

**WILL.** What?

**MIKE.** Say something?

**WILL.** What?

**MIKE.** I don't know, you're always talking, why are you so quiet now?

**WILL.** Umm... *(Looks around.)* ...Everything is in boxes.

**MIKE.** Oh – yup. Told you! UPS guy comes tomorrow.

>  *(Silence.)*

You're so quiet!

**WILL.** Well...put some music on or play your guitar – will you play your guitar?

**MIKE.** It's packed away –

**WILL.** You packed away your guitar?

**MIKE.** It's all got to go.

**WILL.** You should stay here and teach guitar lessons; don't be a doctor! Tell your dad to go fly a kite.

*(Pause.)*

Then let's close our eyes and wish so hard for music that the universe, moved by our determination, will have no other option but to comply.

**MIKE.** That may take years.

**WILL.** Good.

**MIKE.** Okay.

**WILL.** Wait right here.

**MIKE.** Okay.

> *(MIKE laughs and lies back and closes his eyes. WILL does the same. They sit there with their eyes closed until finally, faintly, we hear the opening notes of "Sweet Voice.")*

### [MUSIC NO. 09 "SWEET VOICE"]

> *(MIKE is surprised, it's really just WILL humming.)*
>
> *(They both laugh. WILL hums a little more, and then sings a capella.)*

**WILL.**

SPEAK TO ME WITH YOUR SWEET VOICE
AND TAKE ME THROUGH ANOTHER NIGHT

**MIKE.**

SPEAK TO ME WITH YOUR SOFT VOICE
AND I WILL SURELY BE ALRIGHT.

**MIKE & WILL.**

IF I CAN CLOSE MY EYES WITHOUT A FEAR
SPEAK TO ME WITH YOUR SWEET VOICE NEAR

> *(The BAND begins playing along. During the following, MIKE helps WILL take off his outer shirt. They hold hands. Touch each other's faces. It is sweet.)*

**MIKE, WILL & BACKUPS.**

HOLD ME IN YOUR WARM HAND

**MIKE & BACKUPS.**
    AND I COULD SLEEP WITH YOU TONIGHT
**WILL & BACKUPS.**
    HOLD ME IN YOUR WARM HAND
**MIKE, WILL & BACKUPS.**
    AND I COULD SLEEP WITH YOU TONIGHT

| MIKE & WILL. | BACKUPS. |
|---|---|
| AND ALL MY EARTHLY CARES | OOH |
| MIGHT FADE AWAY | OOH |
| | OOH |

**MIKE & WILL.**
    IF YOU
**MIKE, WILL & BACKUPS.**
    HOLD ME IN YOUR WARM HAND
**MIKE & WILL.**
    THAT WAY
**MIKE.**
    IT'S AS CLOSE AS I GET TO LOVE
**WILL.**
    AS CLOSE AS I GET TO LOVE.

        (**BACKUPS** *echo the following line.*)

**MIKE & WILL.**
    SPEAK TO ME WITH YOUR SWEET VOICE AGAIN

        (**BACKUPS** *echo the following line.*)

    SPEAK TO ME WITH YOUR SWEET VOICE
    AND TAKE ME THROUGH ANOTHER NIGHT
**BACKUPS.**
    SPEAK TO ME WITH YOUR SOFT VOICE
**MIKE, WILL & BACKUPS.**
    AND I WILL SURELY BE ALRIGHT

| MIKE & WILL. | BACKUPS. |
|---|---|
| IF I CAN CLOSE MY EYES | OOH OOH |
| WITHOUT A FEAR | OOH |

(**BACKUPS** *echo the following lines.*)

**MIKE & WILL.**

SPEAK TO ME WITH YOUR SWEET VOICE
SPEAK TO ME WITH YOUR SWEET VOICE
SPEAK TO ME WITH YOUR SWEET VOICE
SPEAK TO ME WITH YOUR SWEET VOICE

*(Music ends.)*

*(The lights slowly fade.)*

## Scene Four

*(It is late the next morning. WILL is sleeping.)*

*(After a moment, WILL wakes up. He slowly realizes he's completely alone in the room. Everything is gone – including MIKE. He is bewildered.)*

WILL. Hello? *(Nothing.)* Hello?

*(Finally, after a long moment of nothing, MIKE enters.)*

MIKE. You're awake!

WILL. Yeah.

MIKE. I overslept. I'm surprised I didn't wake you up – I've been...in and out like a hundred... The UPS guy got here and I didn't have everything ready – the big moving-out day and... *(Suddenly flirty.)* I guess I was distracted. Your hair looks really great right now... I was dreaming about you and about crossword puzzles all night. You were so big in these little boxes. It was funny.

WILL. I didn't dream at all.

MIKE. No, because you were busy crawling around in *mine.*

*(Pause.)*

WILL. It was like the *Twilight Zone* when I woke up. Everything in the room had disappeared. You. Your boxes. Weird.

Have you heard that thing that, like, the most important moment in your life is the first time you realize you're alone in the world – like *on your own*? Oh my God, I think I just had that.

MIKE. Well I had to take care of all of this... *(Smiles.)*

Nothing makes me happier than to know that the very last thing I did in this room was wake up with you after... Okay. Get dressed! It's New Year's Day! Hurry up. We'll grab a bite to eat, you'll come to my game – I'll make sure we hurry up and lose just to get it over with, then we'll, I don't know, ever been to a drive-in?

**WILL.** Do you think it's too late to go to college? Me, I mean?

**MIKE.** *(Laughs.)* Yes.

**WILL.** Oh.

**MIKE.** You have to apply like last year.

**WILL.** Oh. I should figure it out.

**MIKE.** *Yeah.*

**WILL.** Yeah. *(Pause as* **WILL** *considers this.)*

> (**MIKE** *moves to* **WILL** – **WILL** *moves away.* **WILL** *is pensive.)*

It's weird. Like. You. Are. Leaving. Like. *Really.* Like. UPS. Like. I mean. And I'm.

> *(Beat.)*

*(New idea.)* I should have...

> *(Moment.)*

*(New idea.)* Or.

**MIKE.** You okay?

**WILL.** Yeah. I just. How do you...? You know in movies... people look in newspapers and circle...like...jobs...? With a red marker? Is that *real*? Do people... I mean... I think... *(Resolved.)* I'm gonna go home.

**MIKE.** I'll take you.

**WILL.** No. I should. Alone. It's okay.

**MIKE.** Will. Was it...last night... Did I...?

**WILL.** No.

**MIKE.** I didn't mean that you couldn't apply to college. You can.

You should. It's not, like, hard. It was just funny since summer is over.

**WILL.** Yeah, that's funny.

**MIKE.** You're not coming to my game?

**WILL.** I can't.

**MIKE.** But...

**WILL.** I'm going. *FUCK.* Fuck fuck fuck fuck fuck fuck.

> (**WILL** *leaves.)*

## Scene Five

*(WILL walks away – he puts his headphones on. MIKE gets into his car and drives away.)*

### [MUSIC NO. 10 "YOU DON'T LOVE ME"]

**BAND MEMBER 1.**

WHAT A BEAUTIFUL MOMENT
THE TRUTH COMES OUT AT LAST
ONCE YOUR HEART WOULD OWN ME FOREVER
THEN THIS PASSED

AND WHAT A BEAUTIFUL MOMENT
AS MY HEAD COMES APART
DRUNK AND IN A MANNER OF SAYING, WASTED

**BAND MEMBER 1.**

'CAUSE YOU DON'T LOVE ME
YOU DON'T LOVE ME
YOU CAN'T SEE HOW
I MATTER IN THIS WORLD
EVEN THOUGH I LOVE YOU
YOU CAN'T BELIEVE THAT
YOU THINK THAT LEAVING
IS WHAT WILL MAKE YOU HAPPY
THEN I GUESS IT'S OKAY
I THINK IT'S OKAY – IF YOU GO AWAY

*(As the song continues, MIKE parks and goes to play baseball. WILL writes a letter, which he then seals in an envelope and takes to the baseball field. We see WILL approach Mike's car – he sits.)*

| **BAND MEMBER 1.** | **BAND MEMBER 2.** |
|---|---|
| BLOWN RIGHT OUT OF MY SENSES | YOU DON'T KNOW |
| I DID NOT KNOW WHAT TO DO | HOW YOU MOVE ME |
| LOST AND BADLY WANTING SOMEONE | DECONSTRUCT ME |

**BAND MEMBER 1.**

    TO SEE ME THROUGH
    THAT'S WHY I NEEDED
       YOU
    'CAUSE YOU DON'T LOVE
       ME
    YOU DON'T LOVE ME
    YOU CAN'T SEE HOW
    I MATTER IN THIS WORLD
    EVEN THOUGH I LOVE
       YOU
    YOU CAN'T BELIEVE THAT

    IF YOU FIND SOMETHING

    YOU THINK MIGHT MAKE
       YOU HAPPY
    THEN I GUESS IT'S OKAY
    IF YOU GO AWAY
    YOU DON'T LOVE ME
    YOU DON'T LOVE ME
    YOU DON'T LOVE ME

**BAND MEMBER 2.**

    AND CONSUME ME.
    I'M ALL USED UP

    I'M OUT OF LUCK

    I AM!
    BUT I AM SICK OF MYSELF
    WHEN I LOOK AT YOU
    SOMETHING IS BEAUTIFUL
       AND TRUE
    IN A WORLD THAT IS UGLY
       AND A LIE
    ITS HARD TO EVEN WANT
       TO TRY

    I THINK IT'S OKAY
    IF YOU GO AWAY
    YOU DON'T LOVE ME
    YOU DON'T LOVE ME
    YOU DON'T LOVE ME

## Scene Six

> *(When the lights come back up, we are at the baseball field. **WILL** is watching the game from the outfield fence again. Suddenly, **MIKE** runs on, stands in front of **WILL**.)*

**MIKE.** They found your letter. It fell out of my pocket – Mently picked it up.

> *(**MIKE** is horrified. **WILL** looks past **MIKE** and sees that the friends are standing there, watching.)*

Are they...?

> *(**WILL** nods.)*

SO STUPID. GOD! When I stood up it fell out, Mently picked it up, he saw "I Love You." You do? *(Pause.)* I told them...to fuck off, it's just the lyrics to some song.

**WILL.** I was just trying to...

> *(Pause. **MIKE** looks at the boys, then at **WILL**.)*

> *(**MIKE** kisses **WILL**.)*

**MIKE.** *(Almost whispering.)* I'm not even going to turn and look at them because *I don't care* how they're reacting. I care about you. I love you, too.

**WILL.** *(Again – wants to say something, struggles. Finally:)* Then stay.

**MIKE.** Will. You can't expect me to stay here, do you?

> *(Silence.)*

Oh. I'm not staying here.

**WILL.** I know.

**MIKE.** Will.

**WILL.** I didn't really think you were staying. That's why I wrote that stupid note – to say goodbye. Because what else is there to... 'Cause it's time. God! This sucks! Life sucks. It's so mean. Stupid. You're going, that's, like, what happens next... It would be really dumb of me to think anything else might be true. So I don't. I don't. Everyone's going off to school, or back to work, or...like, this big clock has been ticking and...time's up. That's all. And so...like, everyone go on with your life. And you know what your life is, right, you've been paying attention and planning and taking the proper steps, right? And so, I mean, I'm not like...mad...at you... I'm the opposite... I'm just...fucking like really...trying to say goodbye. Now. So... Goodbye. Goodbye. I mean. Goodbye. Michael. I can't. Goodbye.

>    (*Neither of them moves. They just look at each other.*)

>    (**WILL** *goes. Lights fade.*)

## Scene Seven

*(We hear in the darkness: "Ten! Nine! Eight! Seven! Six! Five! Four! Three! Two! One! Happy New Year!" Confetti. It's a New Year's Eve party at a bar/club.)*

### [MUSIC NO. 11 "I WANTED TO TELL YOU"]

*(Time has passed. **WILL** stands in front of the **BAND** watching them play live, in Lincoln, Nebraska. **WILL** shouts to us – over the music – he's having a great time at the concert.)*

**WILL.** They're even better live! I love this song! Happy New Year! I've been in Lincoln for one day – and, and... I'm not gonna go back home! Seriously! I ended up getting a job, by the way – Kmart. I looked up one day when I heard this exact song playing...and I said, "Oh, CRAP! What am I doing?" And then I saw in the newspaper that they were playing live in Lincoln! So, I...I...got on a bus! And here I am...!

> DO JUST WHAT YOU WANT TO
> I THINK YOU'RE RIGHT
> I DO WHAT I WANT TO DO I DO WHAT I WANT TO DO
>
> I LET YOUR WORLD SURROUND ME
> 'CAUSE I SAW NO REAL HARM
> I DIDN'T STOP TO THINK OF YOU
> YOU WERE ALREADY IN MY ARMS
> I WAS WRONG BUT I

**WILL & BACKUPS.**

> I WANTED TO TELL YOU
> I WANTED TO TELL YOU
> WHAT I COULDN'T SAY
> LOVE – I NEEDED TO FIND MINE
> BUT IT TOOK ME A LONG TIME

**WILL.**

> TO SEE.

*(We see* **MIKE**. *He is also at the concert.)*

**MIKE.** *(Re: concert.)* Amazing! A semester of college and I'm already thinking about when I'll be done – or...doing something else. It's alright – I'm glad to be on my own, mostly. School is not... I hate it, okay, I hate it...but I'm here and... I'll figure all of it out! I LOVE THIS SONG!!!

**BACKUPS.**

AHH

**MIKE.**

LOVE –

**MIKE & BACKUPS.**

WELL NEVERMIND

**MIKE.**

I KNOW HOW YOU FEEL ABOUT THAT
NOW

**MIKE & BACKUPS.**

WHAT DO YOU THINK ABOUT TIME?

**BACKUPS.**

SOMETHING...

**MIKE & BACKUPS.**

I WANTED TO TELL YOU
I WANTED TO TELL YOU
WHAT I COULDN'T SAY
LOVE – I NEED TO FIND MINE
AND IT TOOK ME A LONG TIME

**MIKE.**

TO SEE

*(Both* **MIKE** *and* **WILL** *try to move closer to the* **BAND** *– they spot each other.)*

**WILL.** Hey.

**MIKE.** Hey.

*(Neither knows what the other is thinking. They look at each other and sing, still uncertain of how they feel:)*

**MIKE & WILL.**

I DO WHAT I WANT TO DO I DO WHAT I WANT TO DO
I DO WHAT I WANT TO DO I DO WHAT I WANT TO DO

I LET YOUR WORLD SURROUND ME
'CAUSE I SAW NO REAL HARM

**MIKE, WILL & BACKUPS.**

I DIDN'T STOP TO THINK OF YOU

**MIKE & WILL.**

YOU WERE ALREADY IN MY ARMS
I WAS WRONG BUT

*(They give in and start rocking out – thrilled to see each other.)*

**MIKE, WILL & BACKUPS.**

I WANTED TO TELL YOU
I WANTED TO TELL YOU
WHAT I COULDN'T SAY
LOVE – I NEEDED TO FIND MINE

**MIKE & WILL.**

BUT IT

**MIKE, WILL & BACKUPS.**

TOOK ME A LONG TIME

**MIKE & WILL.**

TO SEE

*(They listen to the **BAND** – **MIKE** grabs **WILL**'s hand. The lights fade.)*


**End of Play**


**[MUSIC NO. 12 "BOWS/EXIT MUSIC"]**

www.ingramcontent.com/pod-product-compliance
Lightning Source LLC
Chambersburg PA
CBHW070401120726
47909CB00008B/2941